SLIP STREAM GRAPHICS

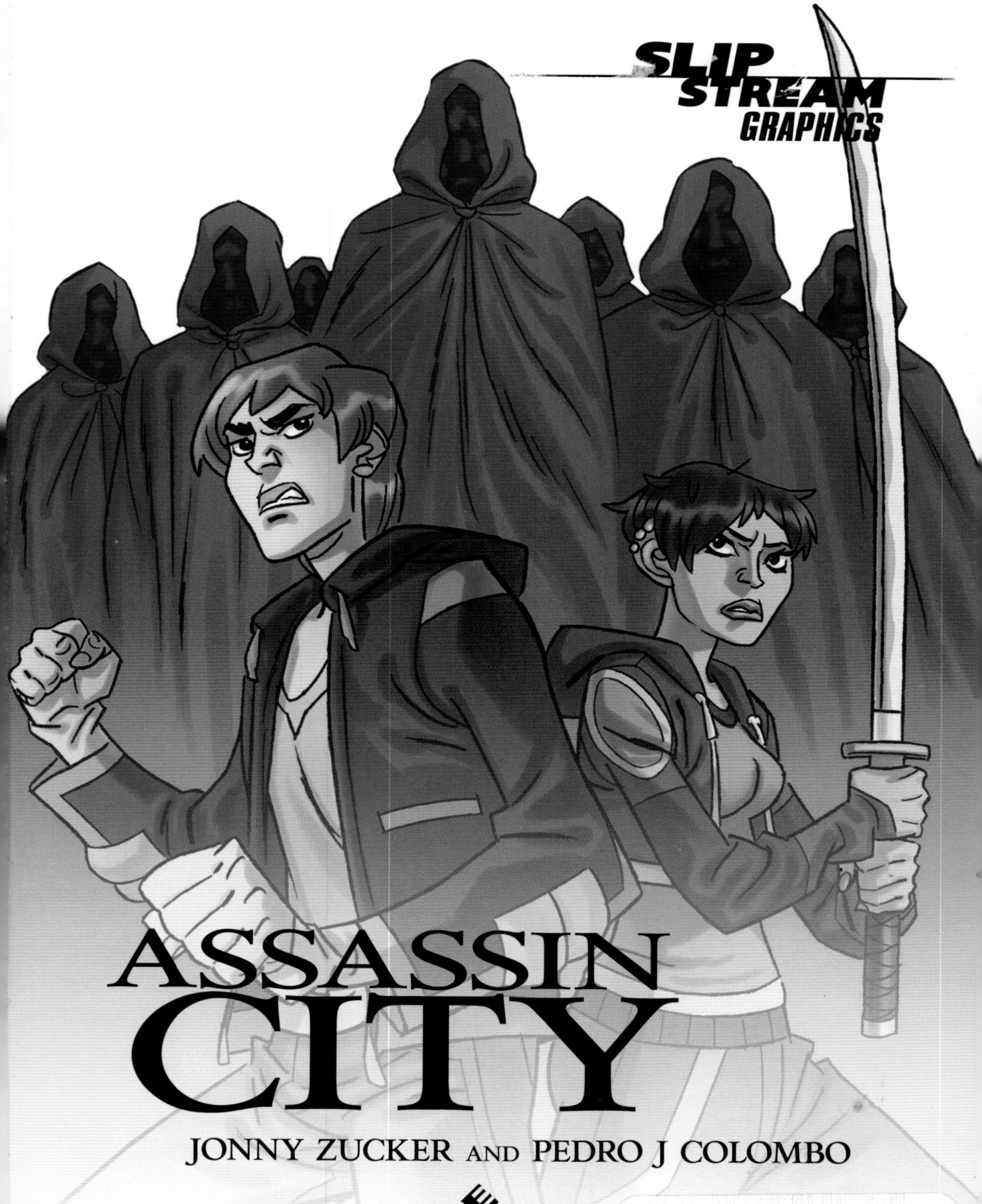

ASSASSIN CITY

JONNY ZUCKER AND PEDRO J COLOMBO

EDGE FRANKLIN WATTS
LONDON•SYDNEY

ASSASSIN CITY

In Alpha City teenagers are summoned to the
Council on their 16th birthday.

The Council gives them a job —
they have no choice.

Today is Milo's 16th birthday...

First published in 2013 by
Franklin Watts
338 Euston Road
London NW1 3BH

Franklin Watts Australia
Level 17/207 Kent Street
Sydney, NSW 2000

Text © Jonny Zucker 2013
Illustrations © Franklin Watts 2013

The rights of Jonny Zucker to be
identified as the author and Pedro J
Colombo as the illustrator of this Work
have been asserted in accordance with the
Copyright, Designs and Patents Act, 1988.

A CIP catalogue record for this book
is available from the British Library.

(ebook) ISBN: 978 1 4451 1809 3
(pb) ISBN: 978 1 4451 1803 1
(Library ebook) ISBN: 978 1 4451 2613 5

Series Editors: Adrian Cole and Jackie Hamley
Series Advisors: Diana Bentley and Dee Reid
Series Designer: Peter Scoulding

A paperback original

1 3 5 7 9 10 8 6 4 2

Printed in China

Franklin Watts is a division of
Hachette Children's Books,
an Hachette UK company
www.hachette.co.uk

NO! I won't do it!

You WILL do your job, or your family will suffer.

You start tomorrow!

The following day...

Welcome to Assassin HQ.

I'm Raff, your combat trainer.

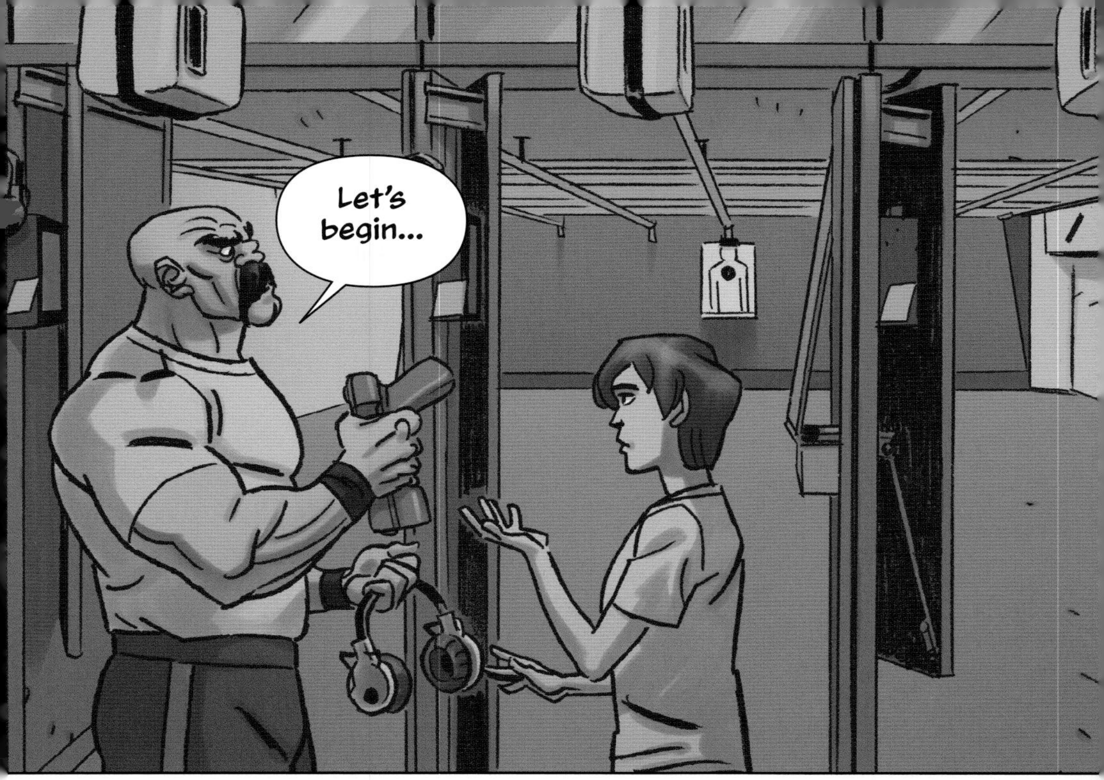
Let's
begin...

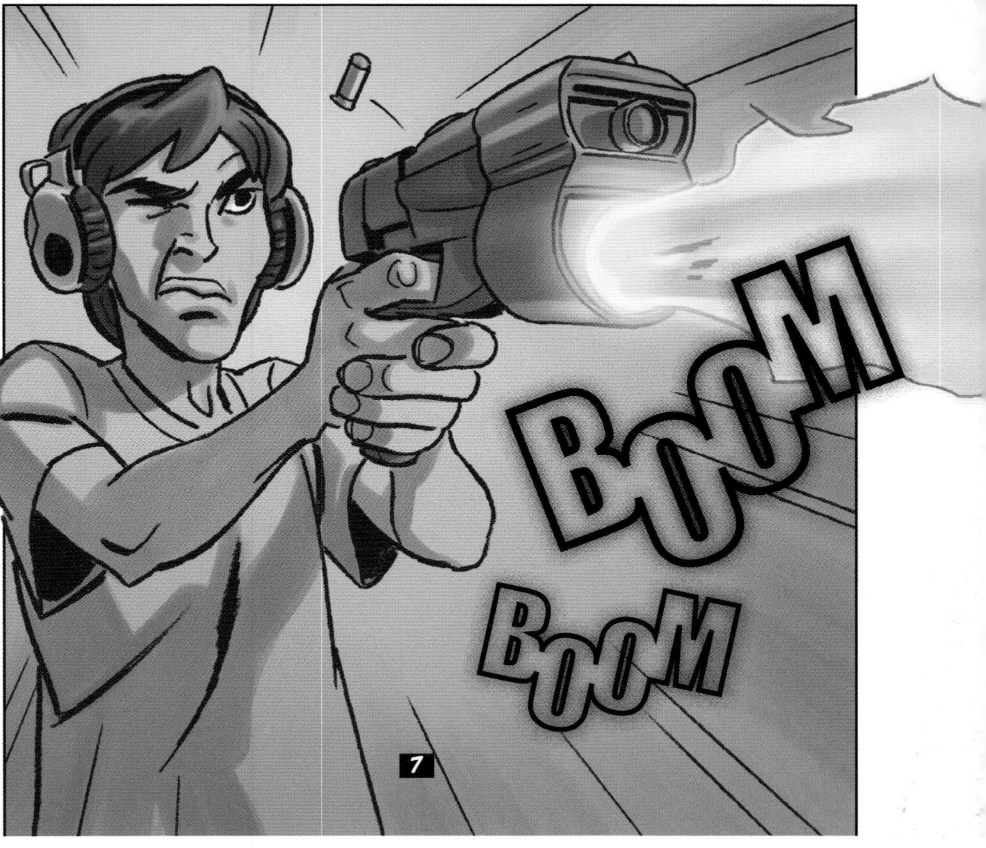
BOOM
BOOM

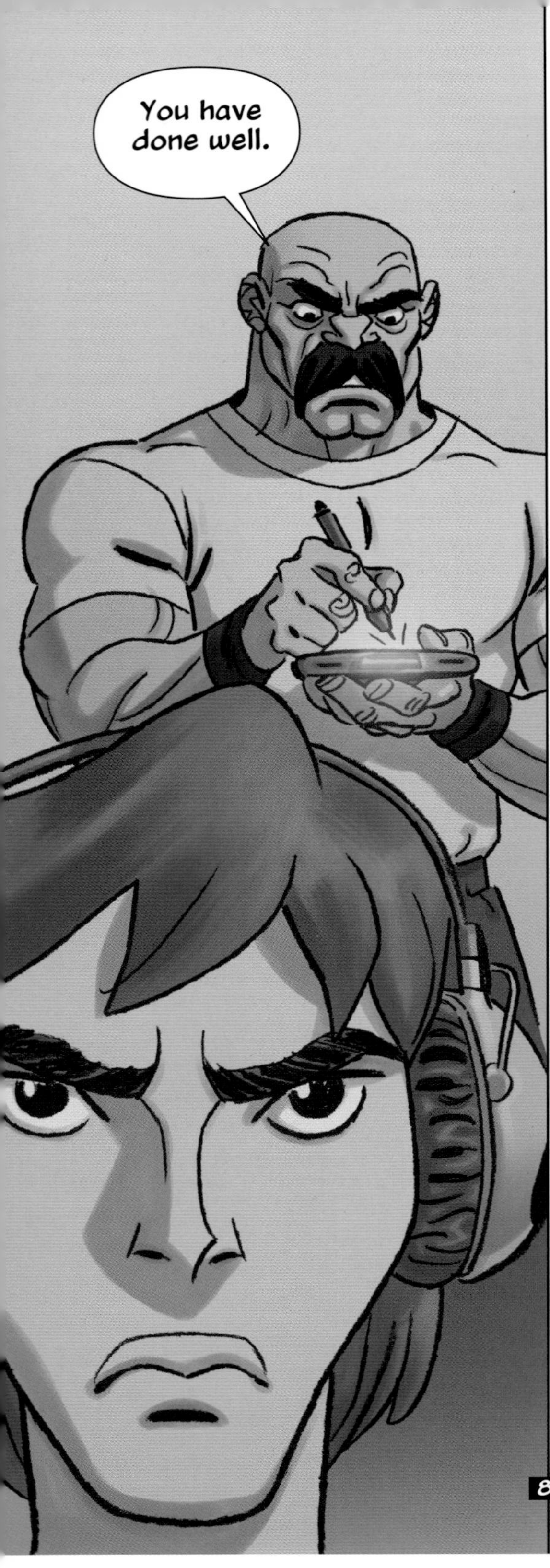
You have done well.

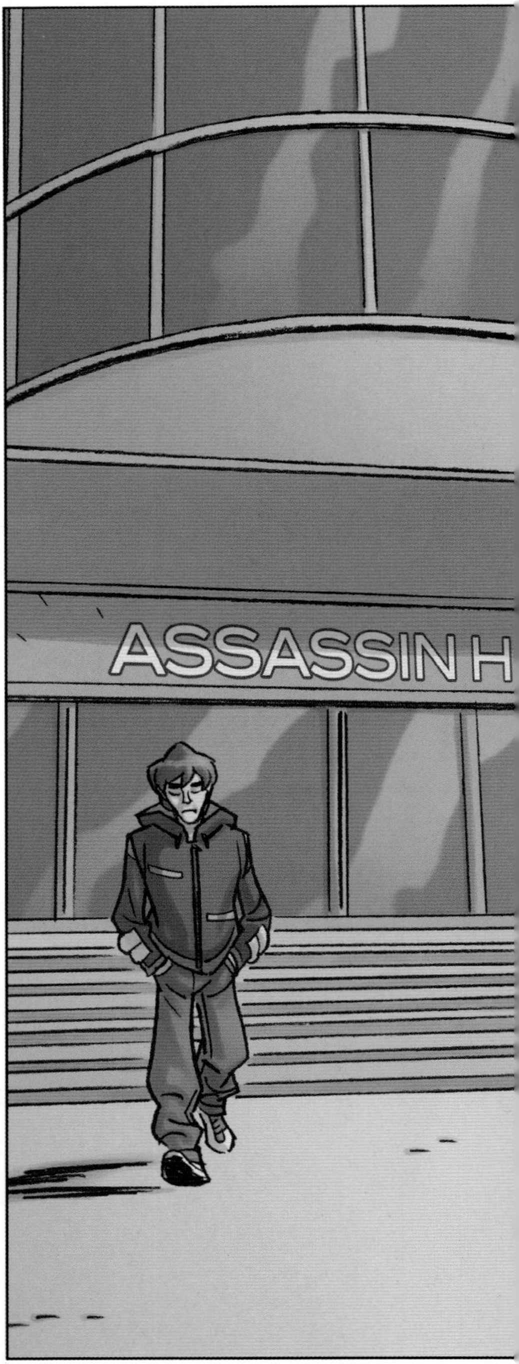
ASSASSIN H

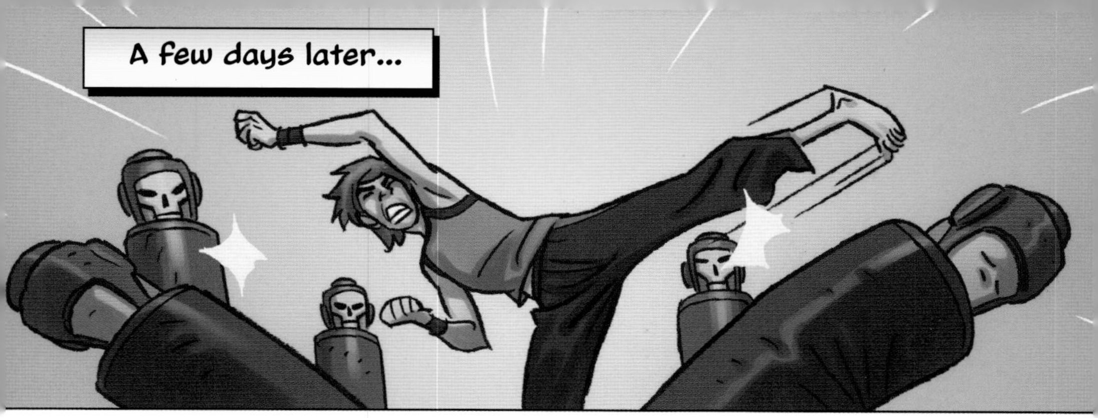
A few days later...

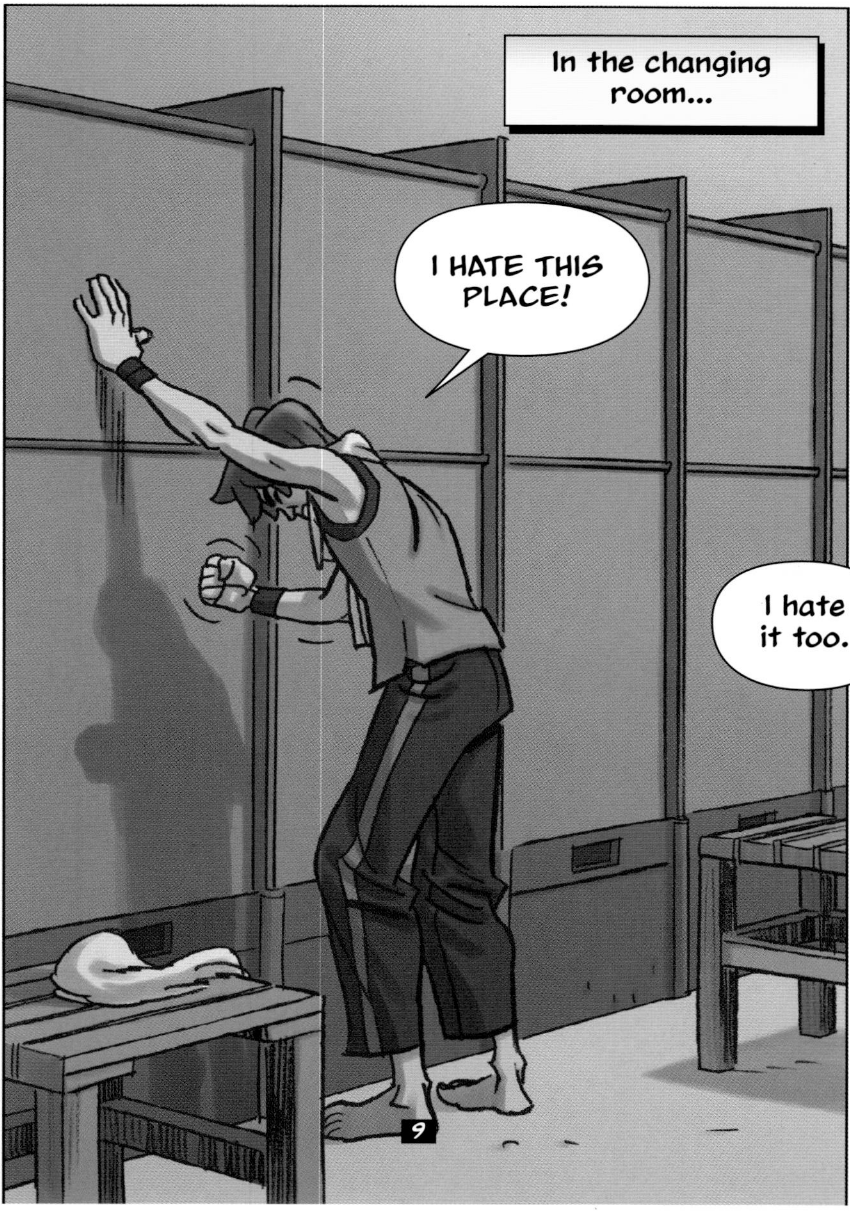
In the changing room...
I HATE THIS PLACE!
I hate it too.

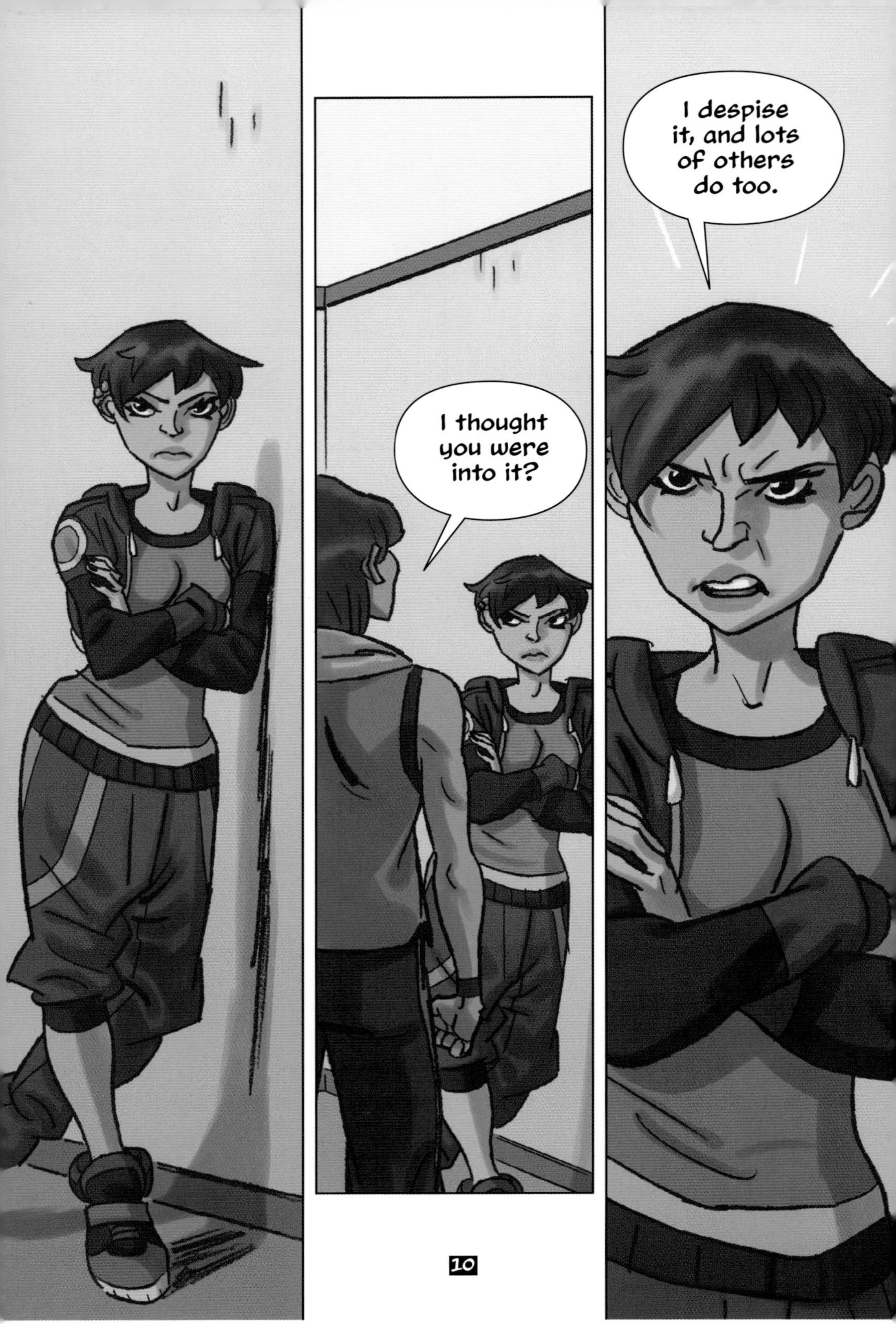
I thought you were into it?
I despise it, and lots of others do too.

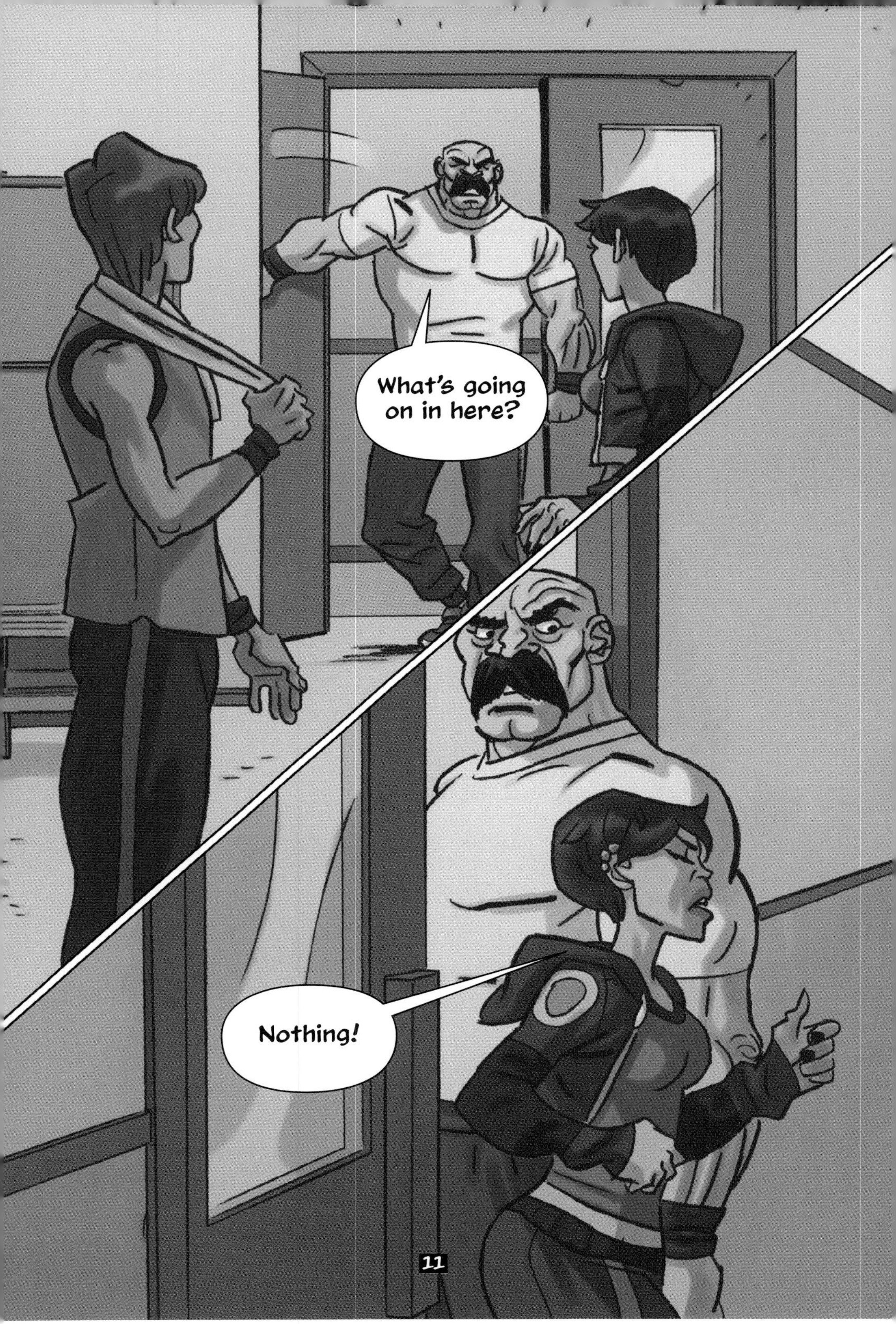
What's going on in here?
Nothing!

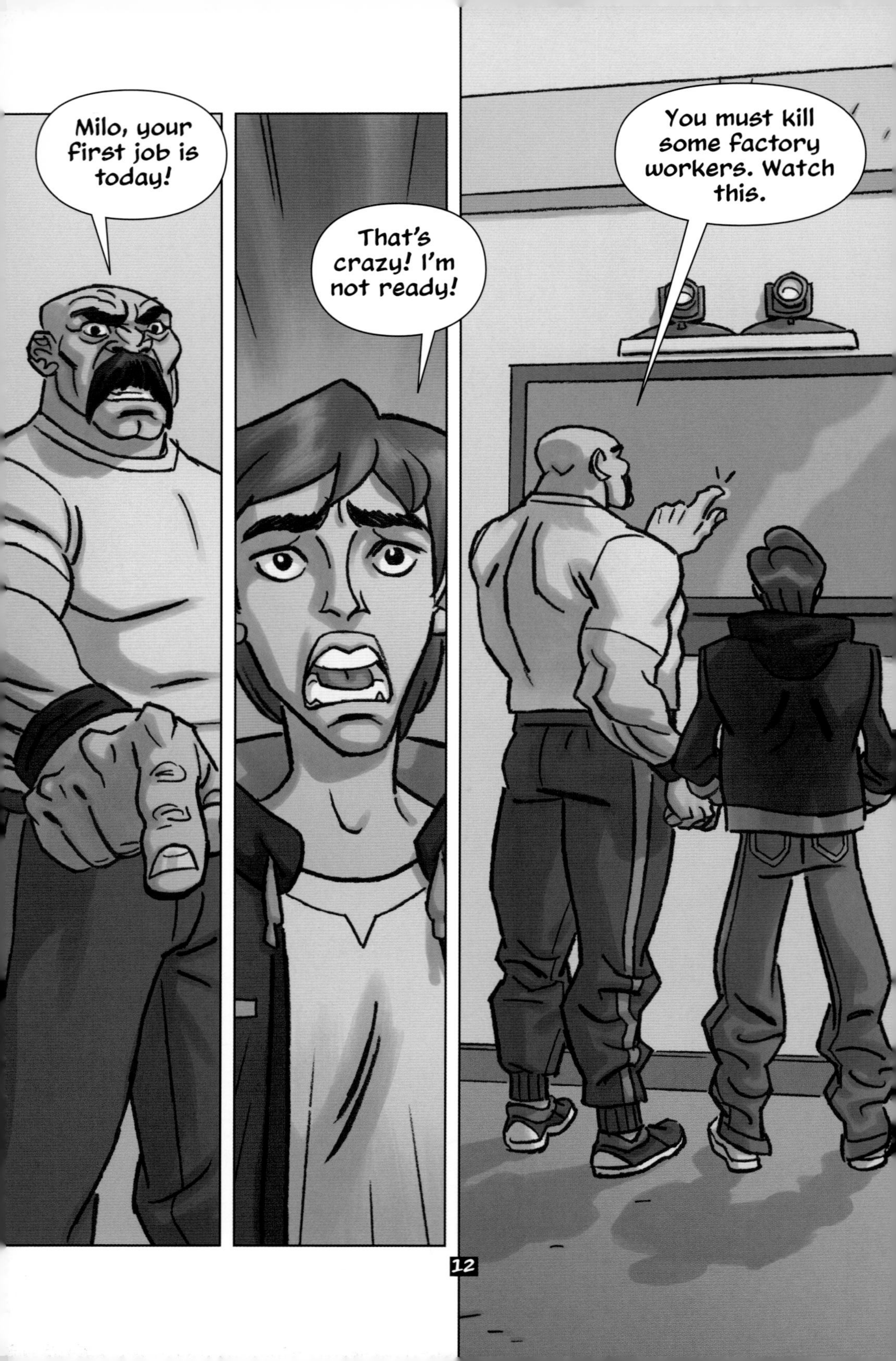
Milo, your first job is today!
That's crazy! I'm not ready!
You must kill some factory workers. Watch this.

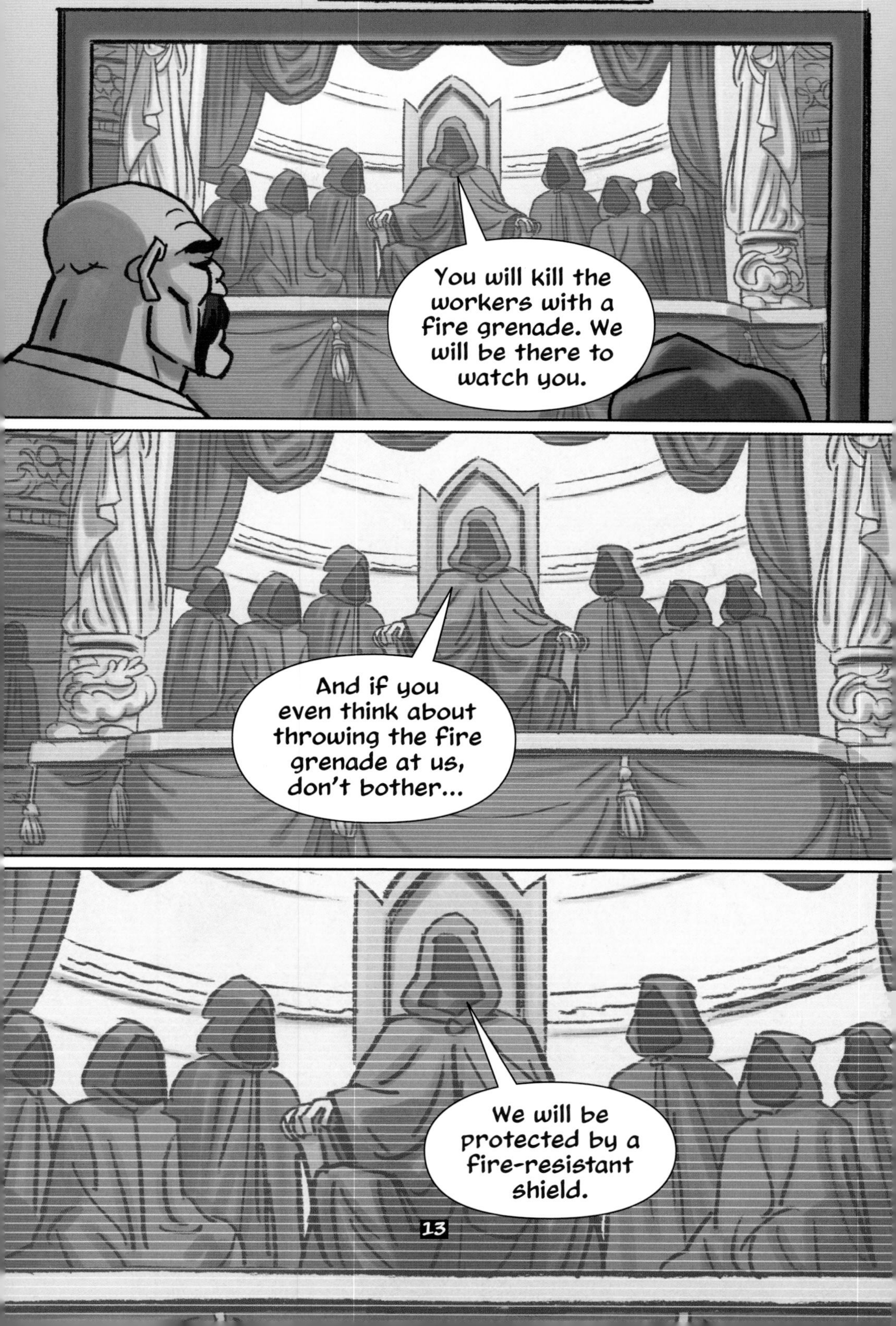

You will kill the workers with a fire grenade. We will be there to watch you.
And if you even think about throwing the fire grenade at us, don't bother...
We will be protected by a fire-resistant shield.

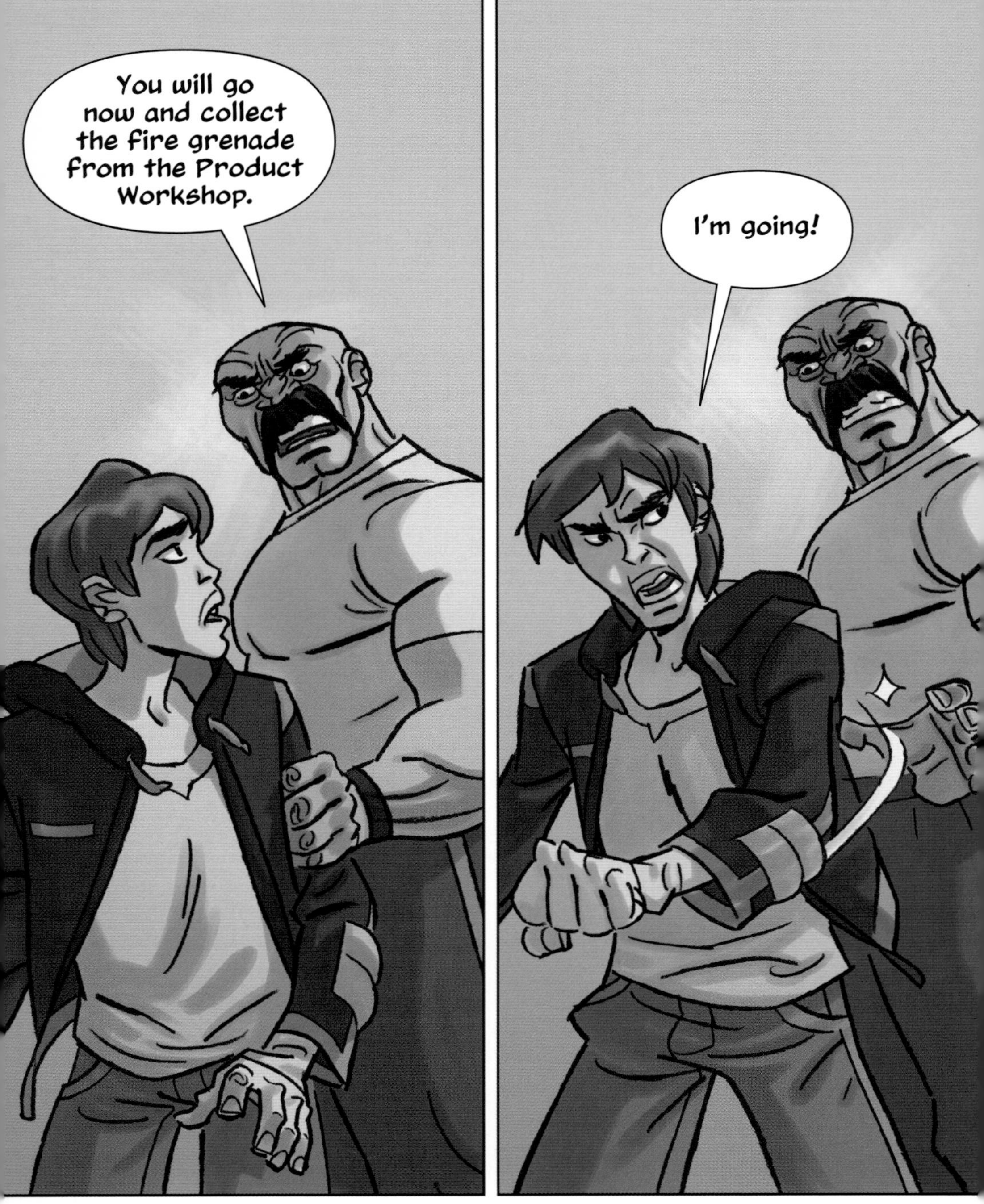
You will go now and collect the fire grenade from the Product Workshop.
I'm going!

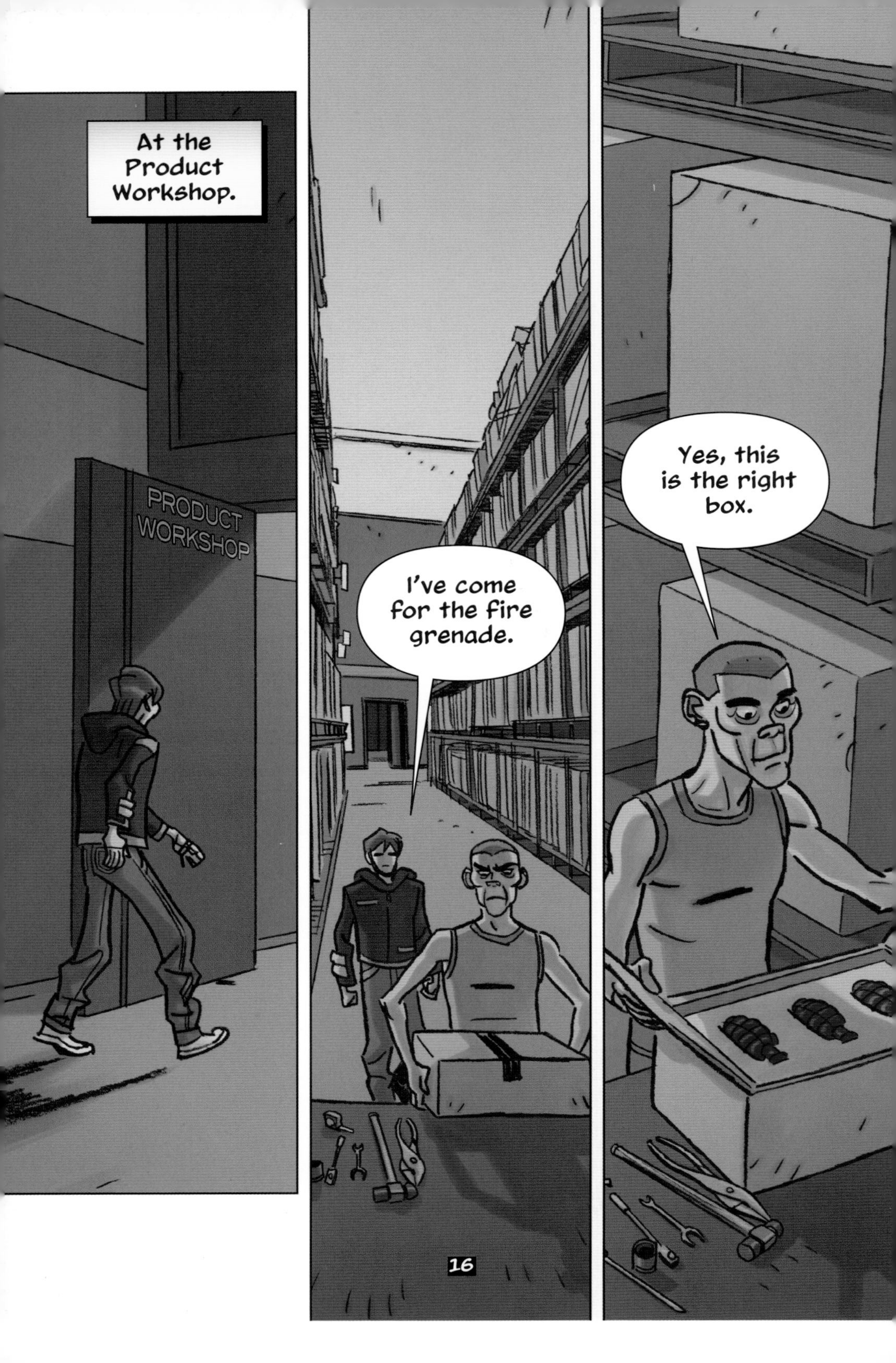
At the Product Workshop.
PRODUCT WORKSHOP
I've come for the fire grenade.
Yes, this is the right box.

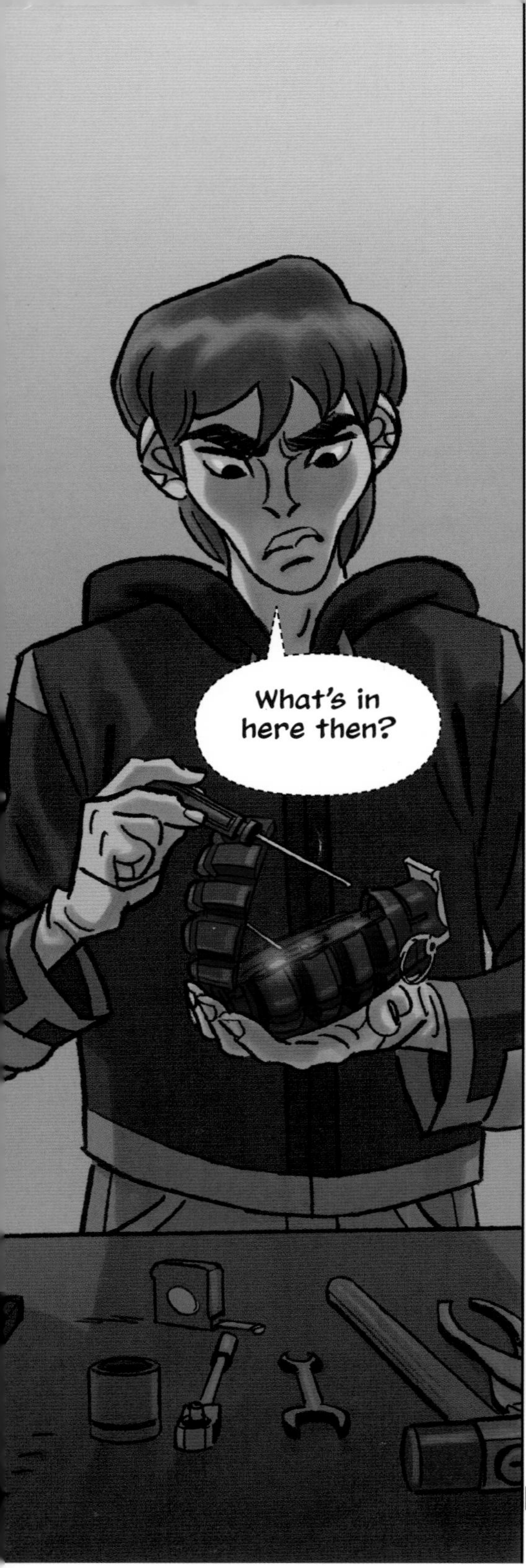
What's in here then?
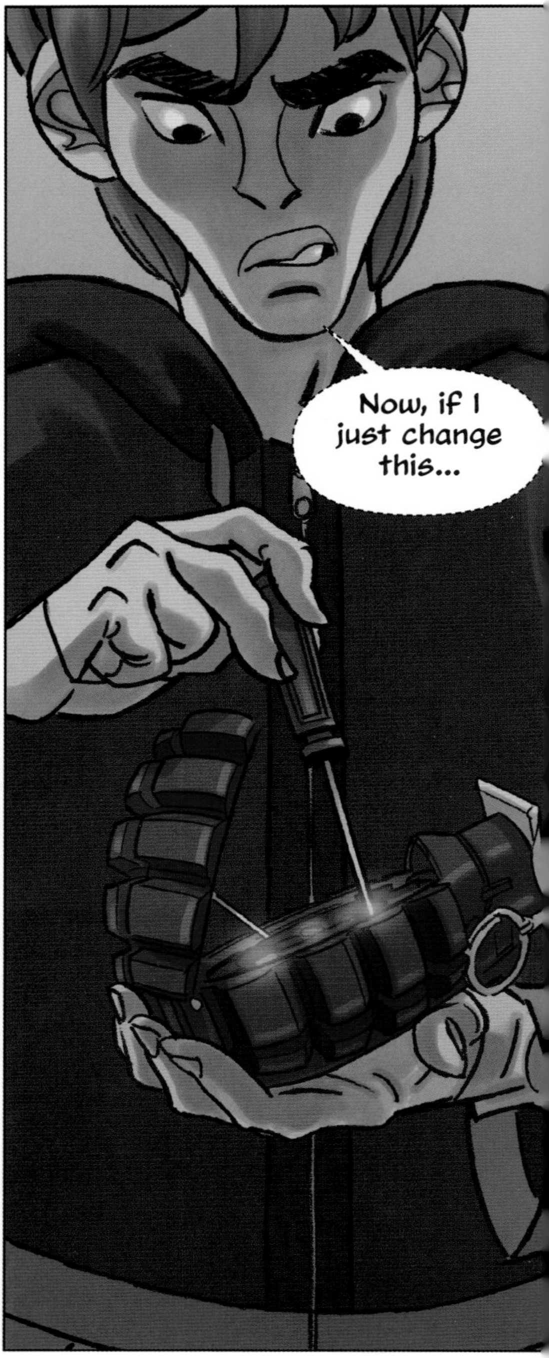
Now, if I just change this...

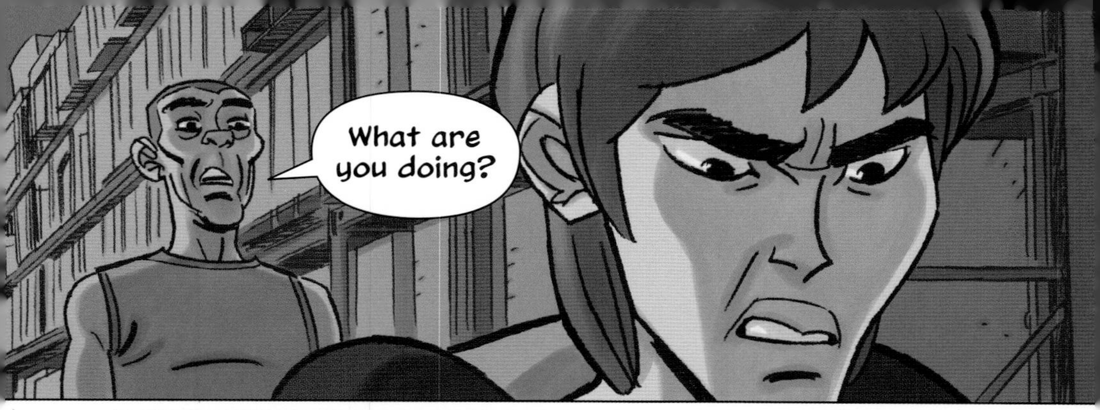
What are you doing?

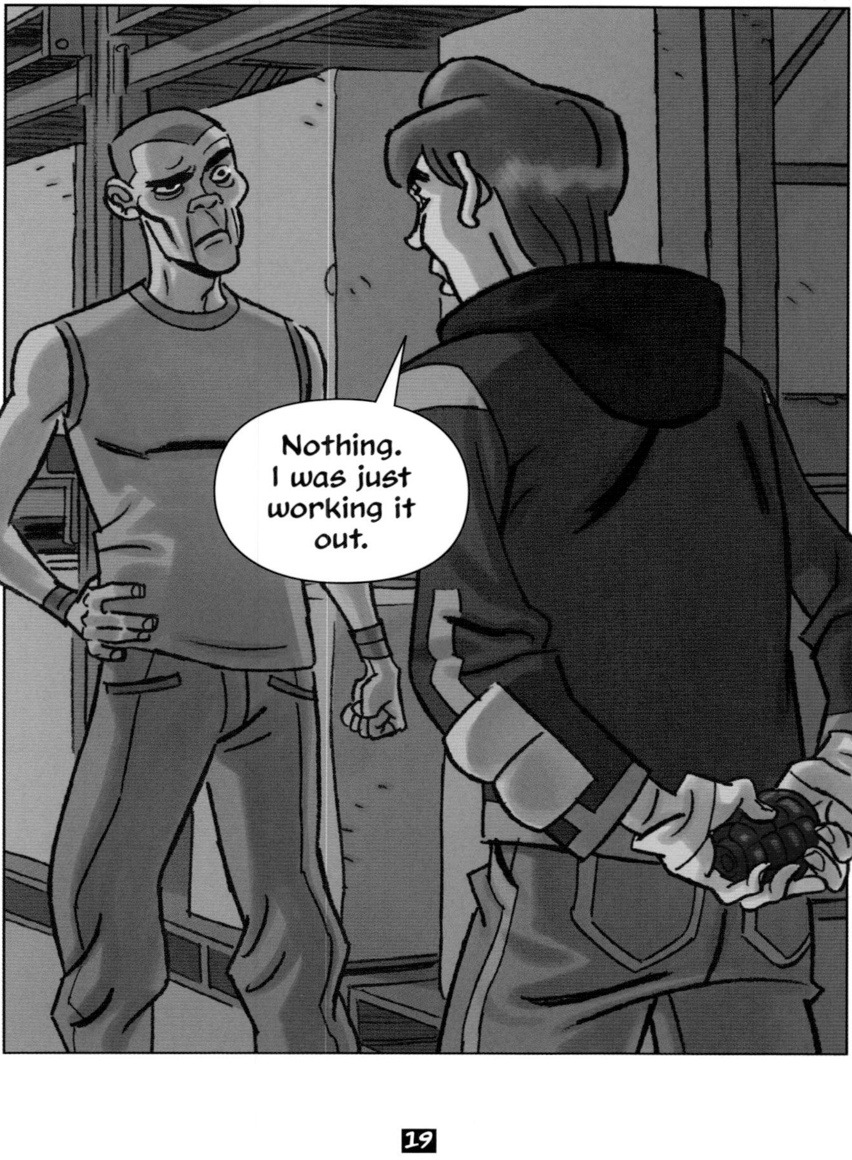
Nothing. I was just working it out.

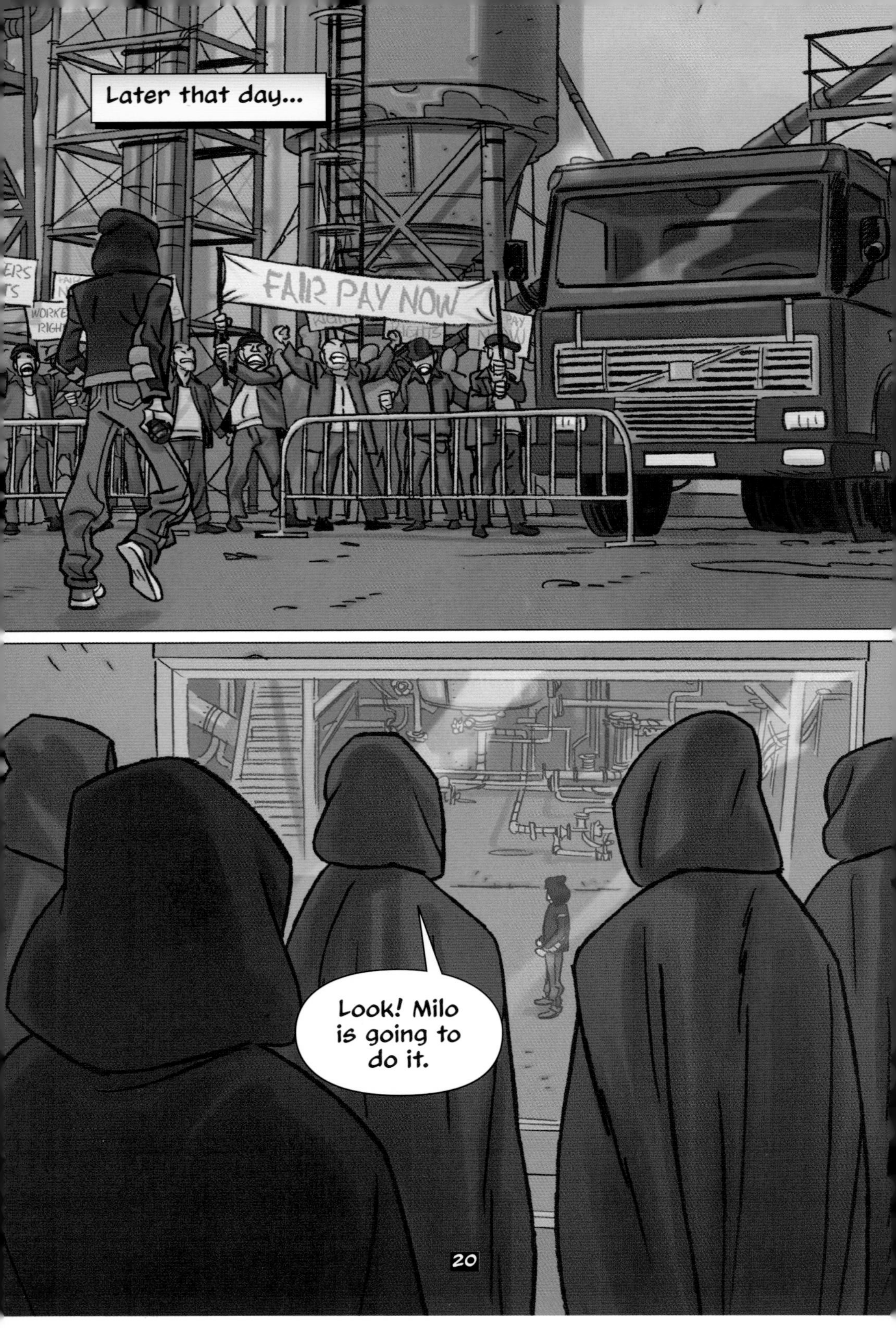
Later that day...
FAIR PAY NOW
Look! Milo is going to do it.

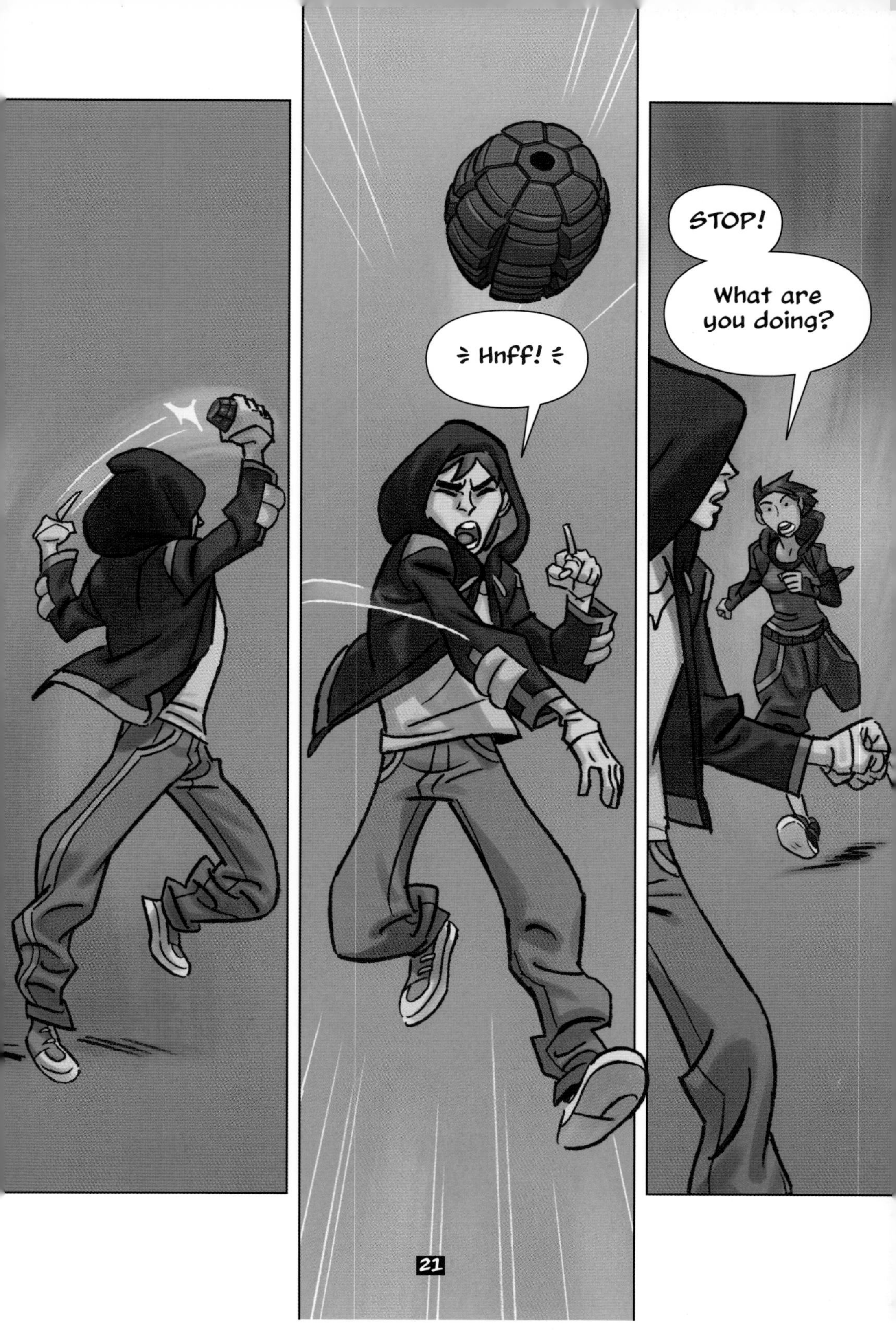

Hnff!
STOP!
What are you doing?

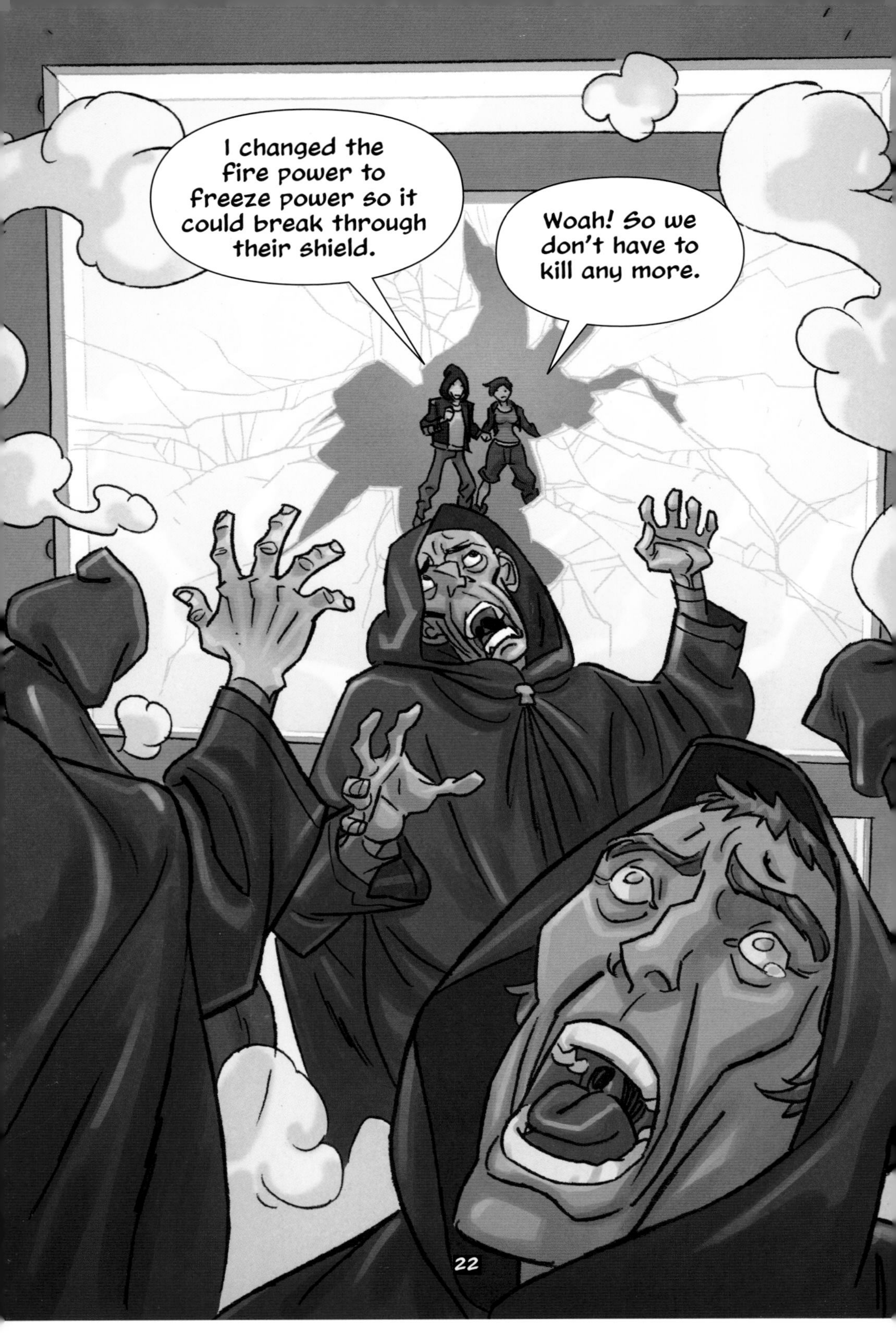
I changed the fire power to freeze power so it could break through their shield.
Woah! So we don't have to kill any more.

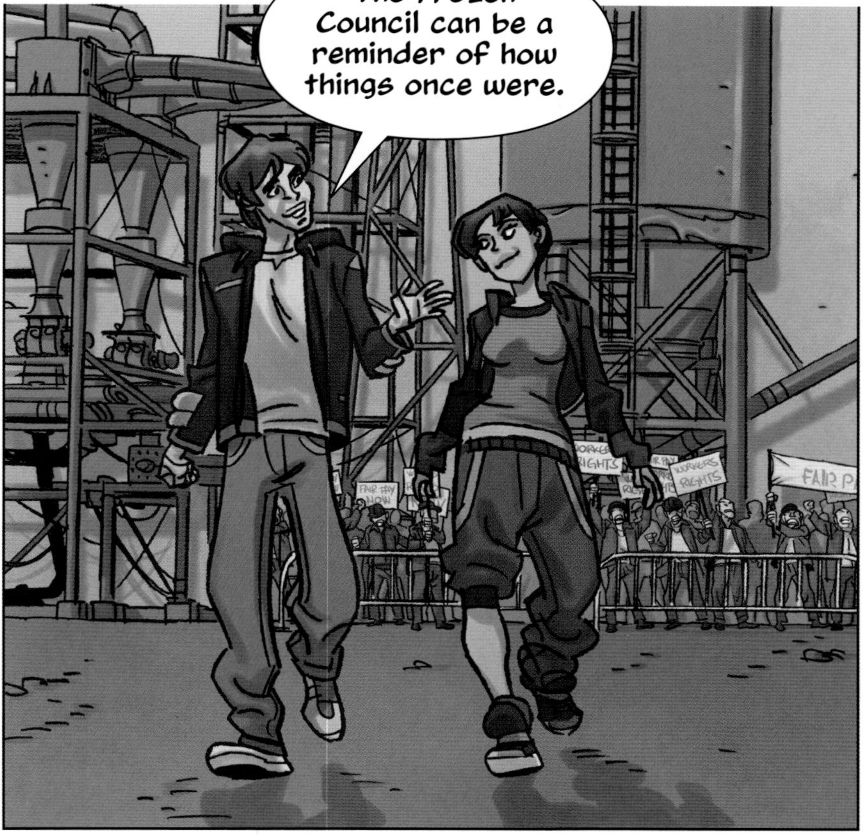
The frozen Council can be a reminder of how things once were.
WORKERS RIGHTS

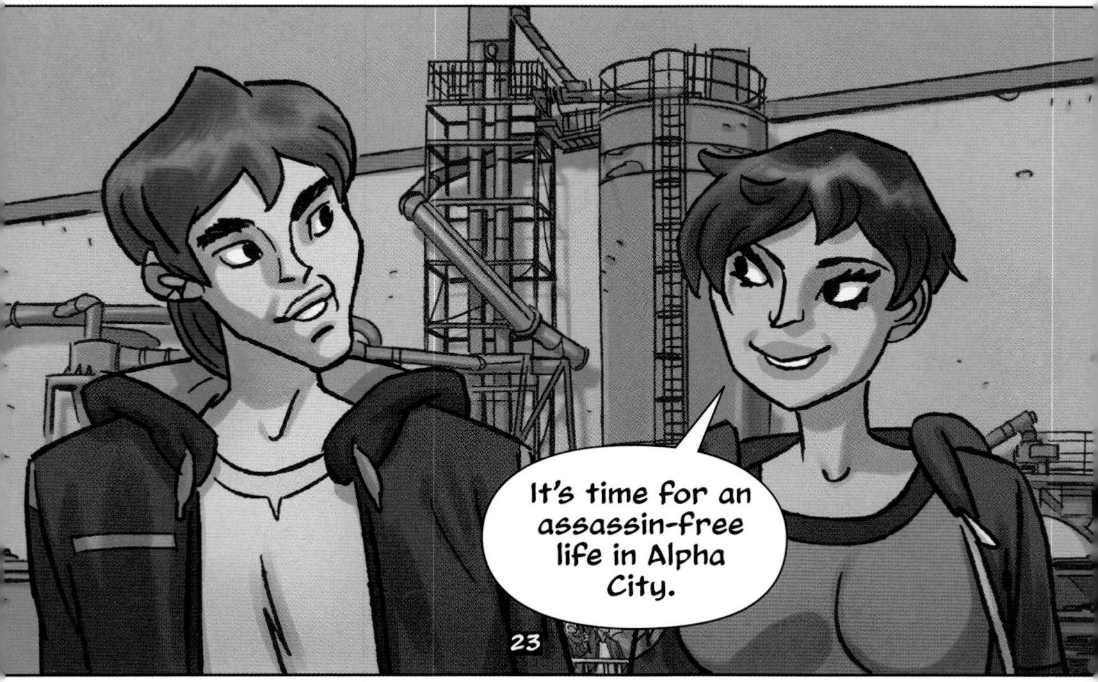
It's time for an assassin-free life in Alpha City.

FOR TEACHERS

About SLIP STREAM

Slipstream is a series of expertly levelled books designed for pupils who are struggling with reading. Its unique three-strand approach through fiction, graphic fiction and non-fiction gives pupils a rich reading experience that will accelerate their progress and close the reading gap.

At the heart of every Slipstream graphic fiction book is a great story. Easily accessible words and phrases ensure that pupils both decode and comprehend, and the high interest stories really engage older struggling readers.

Whether you're using Slipstream Level 1 for Guided Reading or as an independent read, here are some suggestions:

1. Make each reading session successful. Talk about the text or pictures before the pupil starts reading. Introduce any unfamiliar vocabulary.

2. Encourage the pupil to talk about the book using a range of open questions. For example, how would they feel if they were given the job of an assassin?

3. Discuss the differences between reading fiction, graphic fiction and non-fiction. What do they prefer?

Slipstream Level 1 photocopiable **WORKBOOK**
ISBN: 978 1 4451 1798 0
available – download free sample worksheets from:
www.franklinwatts.co.uk

For guidance, SLIPSTREAM Level 1 – Assassin City has been approximately measured to:

National Curriculum Level: 2c
Reading Age: 7.0–7.6
Book Band: Turquoise

ATOS: 1.7*
Guided Reading Level: H
Lexile® Measure (confirmed): 220L

*Please check actual Accelerated Reader™ book level and quiz availability at www.arbookfind.co.uk